MUSEUM MYSTERIES

W I D

Spies & Detectives

Raintree is an imprint of Capstone Global Library Limited, a company incorporated in England and Wales having its registered office at 7 Pilgrim Street, London, EC4V 6LB – Registered company number: 6695582

www.raintree.co.uk
myorders@raintree.co.uk

Printed and bound in China.

ISBN 978-1-4062-9412-5
18 17 16 15 14
10 9 8 7 6 5 4 3 2 1

British Library Cataloguing in Publication Data
A full catalogue record for this book is available from the British Library.

Every effort has been made to contact copyright holders of material reproduced in this book. Any omissions will be rectified in subsequent printings if notice is given to the publisher.

All the internet addresses (URLs) given in this book were valid at the time of going to press. However, due to the dynamic nature of the internet, some addresses may have ~~changed or ceased to exist since publication. While the author~~ use readers, no responsibility for any ~~~~ or the publisher.

backgrounds, paper textures); NASA
ohs Division (Wright brothers flight)

The case of the
MISSING MUSEUM
ARCHIVES

By Steve Brezenoff
Illustrated by Lisa K. Weber

raintree
a Capstone company — publishers for children

Fact Sheet:
German "Bat-Wing" Plane

Physical Description: WWII; twin-jet engines; delta shape; steel fuselage with wood coverage

Country of Origin: Germany

Manufacturer: Horten, Reimar and Walter

Wingspan: 16.8 m (55.4 ft)

Length: 7.47 m (24.6 ft)

Height: 2.81 m (9.3 ft)

Weights: 5,067 kg (11,198 lb)

Engines: (2) Junkers-Jumo 004 B-2 turbojet

<u>Notes:</u> Considered the first stealth plane. Test flights had multiple crashes. Design abandoned.

Amal Farah

Raining Sam

Wilson Kipper

Clementine Wim

Capitol City Sleuths

Amal Farah
Age: 11
Favourite Museum: Air and Space Museum
Interests: astronomy, space travel and
building models of space ships

Raining Sam
Age: 12
Favourite Museum: History Museum
Interests: Ojibwe history, culture and
traditions, history – good and bad

Clementine Wim
Age: 13
Favourite Museum: The Museum of Art
Interests: painting, sculpting with clay and
anything colourful

Wilson Kipper
Age: 10
Favourite Museum: Natural History Museum
Interests: dinosaurs (especially pterosaurs
and herbivores) and building dinosaur models

TABLE OF

CONTENTS

CHAPTER 1
Running late

Eleven-year-old Amal Farah lay on her back on the floor of her bedroom. Even though it was just after breakfast and the sun was shining brightly outside, Amal gazed up at the stars and planets – a solar system mobile and glow-in-the-dark stars on her bedroom ceiling.

"Amal?" said a voice near her head. "Hello? Earth to Amal?" It was Raining Sam, one of her best friends, talking on the phone. She'd completely tuned out.

Amal would never forget the first time she'd heard Raining Sam's name. She and her father, Dr Ahmed Farah, had just moved to Capitol City because he had taken a new job at the Air and Space Museum. Raining had been one of the first kids she'd met when they arrived.

Raining's mother had just started at the American History Museum, which was run by the same non-profit organization as the Air and Space Museum. He'd accompanied his mother on the museum tour, just as Amal had accompanied her father.

During dinner that night, Amal had laughed and said, "Raining Sam? Is that a name or a weather forecast?"

She'd meant it as a joke, but her father hadn't been amused. "A lot of people you meet in Capitol City might think our Somali names are pretty funny too," he'd said with a pointed look.

Amal knew just what he meant. That had been only a few weeks ago. Since then, Amal and Raining had become close friends. She'd quickly learned that he knew almost nothing about astronomy, her favourite subject, but he was very interested in Ojibwe – the name of his tribe of indigenous people.

And Amal hadn't laughed at his name even once since then.

"Sorry," she apologized. "I called to see if you want to come with me to the Air and Space Museum today. Dad's going to let me stay there today while he's working."

Raining didn't answer. Instead, he moved the phone away from his mouth and shouted, "Mum! Can I spend the day with Amal today at the Air and Space Museum?" A moment later he said into the phone, "She says I can."

"Great!" Amal replied happily. "We'll pick you up. And don't worry about bringing lunch. Dad will get us free food in the canteen."

"Burgers?" Raining asked.

"Whatever you want, I suppose," Amal said. "See you soon."

Amal jumped to her feet, shoved her phone into the pocket of her jeans and grabbed her favourite headscarf from the chair at her desk.

Her dad was always telling her she needed to do a better job of keeping her scarves more organized so they wouldn't always be wrinkled or lost. But what was the point? This dark blue one, with a pattern of gold stars, was the only one she ever wanted to wear anyway.

"I'm ready, Dad," Amal said as she hurried down the stairs.

Her father stood at the front door tapping his foot. His museum badge hung from his shirt pocket. "Finally," he said impatiently. "Hurry up and get in the car. We'll be late!"

"We have to pick up Raining on the way," Amal said quickly as she dashed through the open front door and flashed a grin at her dad. "Hurry, hurry!"

CHAPTER 2
Who was that?

They made it to the museum on time, but only just. When they hurried in, Amal spotted the museum's head archivist, Dr Helga Heinfeld, leaning on the museum's front desk, as if she had been waiting for her assistant to arrive.

"I'm very sorry, Dr Heinfeld," Amal's father said to his boss.

Dr Heinfeld smiled, though, not at all angry. "You're right on time, Ahmed," she said. "I have a morning meeting with some very important donors, so I have to be off. You can handle your duties in the office without my supervision, can't you?"

"Of course, Dr Heinfeld," said Dr Farah, smiling too. "That won't be a problem at all."

"Great!" said Dr Heinfeld. She patted Amal on the head, grabbed her bag from the desk and slipped through the museum's revolving front door.

Amal adjusted her hijab and watched the doctor strut away. She hated it when grown-ups patted her head.

"What's an important donor?" Raining asked.

Dr Farah leaned across the front desk to grab two temporary badges for the children. "That means people who give a lot of money to the museum," he said. "Or people who donate items for exhibitions."

"Why does your boss have a meeting with them?" Amal asked.

"It's part of her job," her father explained. "Now I have to get to my office. You two enjoy the museum. I'll meet you back here at midday for lunch."

"Okay," Amal agreed. She grabbed Raining's hand and pulled her friend deeper into the museum. "Let's start at the shuttle missions exhibition."

"Oh, good idea," said Raining. "We can learn about Commander John Herrington."

"Was he an astronaut?" Amal asked. She knew a lot about space, and just like everyone else, she knew the famous astronauts. But even *she* didn't know every name from every mission. She was surprised Raining knew any of them.

"Mm," Raining said, nodding. They stepped through a lit archway and walked into a big room. It was still early, and the room was lit only by the lights along the wall and around exhibition cases in the centre of the space. "And he's a member of the Chickasaw Nation."

Amal shot him a confused glance. "A member of the what?" she asked.

"He's American Indian," Raining explained. "Like me. He's just from a different tribe."

"I don't think I saw anything about him last week," Amal said. Dr Heinfeld had given her and her father a full tour of the museum before he started.

Raining moved over to the first illuminated exhibit. It showed photos of *Sputnik*, the Russian satellite, and the first American satellite, *Explorer 1*.

"NASA was founded right after that," Amal said as she came to a stop next to her friend.

Raining nodded. "Herrington was about forty years later," he said. He hurried along the room, skipping past the displays on the Mercury Program, the Gemini Program, *Apollo* and Skylab. He finally stopped five lighted exhibits further along, and pointed. "Here he is."

Amal hurried over to join him. On top of the display case, lit by a spotlight high in the ceiling, stood a model of the International Space Station. The centre of the model was made up of a bunch of white tubes, with long, black rectangles sticking off it, like wings.

"Herrington was a mission specialist in 2002," Raining said, squinting at the backlit display on one side.

Amal circled the exhibit. It highlighted the shuttle flights to the ISS from 1998 to the present day. "Cool," she said. "So what should we do next? Maybe there's a film we can see at the cinema or a show at the planetarium."

Raining shrugged. "Whatever you want to do," he said.

"Wait a sec," Amal said. "I've got the programme somewhere." From her back pocket she pulled out all the leaflets and brochures she'd gathered since the last time her jeans had been washed. They fell into a heap on the floor.

"Bother," she said. She and Raining dropped to their knees to scoop up the paper.

"Is this it?" Raining asked. He held a glossy, folded brochure out to Amal.

Amal took the brochure from him and squinted at it. She couldn't see very well in the dim lighting, but she spotted a couple of familiar images: space ships and rockets and shadowy pictures of ringed planets and cratered moons. Definitely not the cinema programme.

"Oh!" she said as the answer struck her. "I totally forgot. I grabbed this from the hotel."

"Hotel?" Raining repeated.

Amal nodded. "Dad and I stayed in a hotel for two nights before we moved into our flat," she explained. "The reception area had all sorts of brochures. This one is for a space-themed amusement park."

Raining nodded. "Oh, yes. Francis's Flying Funland," he said. "I saw the signs on the motorway. It's only here for a few weeks."

"We should go soon, then," Amal suggested.

"Okay," Raining agreed. He gathered up the papers on the floor and handed the pile to Amal.

"Here it is," Amal said, spotting the programme on top of the pile. She squinted at the timings. "Let's find somewhere with a bit more light."

The two friends stood up from the dark, carpeted floor and found the nearest lit doorway. It led to the retired space shuttle, which was on display in a huge, sunlit room. Raining whistled at the impressive ship.

"Pretty cool, eh?" Amal said. "It's the first ever reusable space ship, and it's more than 35 metres long."

Raining nodded with his mouth open in amazement.

"This ship will be remembered as the grandfather of all viable space travel," Amal continued.

"Viable?" Raining repeated, sounding confused.

"It means likely to succeed," Amal said. "Anyway, let's see which films are showing."

The two friends stood close together to look at the film times. Just then, Amal heard the clip-clop of high-heeled shoes echoing through the hall. From behind the massive body of the orbiter, she could just see a pair of black shoes and black trousers walk quickly and calmly through the room.

Forgetting about the cinema programme, Amal hurried over to the other side of the orbiter just in time to see whoever it was vanish into the darkness of the NASA-timeline display.

"Wasn't that your father's boss?" Raining asked, coming over to Amal.

"I don't know," she said. "I didn't really get a good look. It must have been, though. Who else would be walking through the museum as if they own the place?"

"Is it even open yet?" Raining asked.

Just then, the speaker system crackled to life, and a voice rang through the museum. "Good morning, visitors," said Jimmy, the museum's head of security. He launched into his daily announcement, the same one he made every morning, about the museum's rules and regulations.

"It's open now," Amal said. "But what would Dr Heinfeld be doing in here? She said she had to leave."

"And we *saw* her leave," Raining pointed out.

"Weird," Amal said. Then she shrugged. "So, film?"

CHAPTER 3
Missing plans

Amal and Raining caught the planetarium show about Mars, which also discussed how people might one day travel to the red planet.

"Sounds impossible," Raining said as they left the planetarium.

"No way," Amal argued. "Nothing's impossible. We'll find a way to do it."

"You're so sure?" Raining said.

Amal nodded. "I intend to go there myself one day," she said.

Raining chuckled a little. Amal might have been offended, but at the next corner she bumped right into her father.

"Oh!" Dr Farah said, surprised. "I didn't see you." His face was flushed and he was short of breath.

"Are you okay?" Amal asked.

"I … I'm fine," her father said. "A minor office emergency. Nothing to worry about."

"Okay," Amal said. "Almost lunchtime, isn't it?"

"What?" her father said. "Lunchtime? Well, enjoy!" Then he started to walk off.

"Hey, Dad," Amal said, grabbing his wrist. "You're eating with me and Raining, remember?"

Her father barely seemed to hear her. "Is it raining? What a shame. Bye now." With that, he hurried off down the corridor towards the management offices.

"What do you think happened?" Raining asked.

"I don't know," Amal said. "But we better follow him."

"You think that's a good idea?" her friend asked.

"If we don't follow him, we won't get any lunch," Amal said. "What choice do we have?"

* * *

"I'm waiting for an explanation, Ahmed," a woman's voice said, sounding angry.

Amal and Raining stood just outside the door to her father's office. They would have followed him inside, but then they had heard Dr Heinfeld. She didn't sound happy.

"Those plans were very hard to get," Dr Heinfeld shouted. "I travelled to Austria and hiked through the Ötztal Alps to find a man who was 107 years old, lying on his death bed."

"I know," Dr Farah said. "I'm – "

"And do you know what he said to me?" Dr Heinfeld interrupted.

"No," said Dr Farah.

"Neither do I," Dr Heinfeld snapped. "He only spoke Friulian. I've never even *heard* of Friulian. But he sold me these plans at great cost – to our gracious donors, of course."

"Well, I'm sure that – " Dr Farah started to say.

"How will I explain to the donors that my new assistant has lost them?" Dr Heinfeld roared.

"But, Doctor – " said Amal's father.

But Dr Heinfeld refused to let him get a word in. "No more excuses!" she snapped. "Find those plans or this will be your last day working at this museum!"

Angry footsteps stamped towards the door, and Amal and Raining hurried around the corner to hide.

As soon as Dr Heinfeld's clumping footsteps were far away, Amal and Raining hurried back to Dr Farah's office. He sat with his face down onto his folded arms on his desk. "This is bad," he muttered to himself. "This is very, very bad."

"Dad?" Amal said, moving slowly closer to her father.

Dr Farah jerked his head up quickly and gave a false smile. "Amal!" he said. "How nice to see you." He started to get up. "Are you kids ready for lunch?"

"Dad," Amal said, walking over to the desk and putting a hand on his arm. "We, er, overheard Dr Heinfeld."

"What?" her father said, still smiling and pretending nothing was wrong. But he could tell it wasn't working. After a brief moment, he dropped back into his chair and dropped his head onto the desk again. "I don't know what to do."

"Did you really lose that thing she was talking about?" Raining asked from the doorway.

Dr Farah shrugged. "I don't even know anymore," he said. "I did some work in the archives this morning, but I don't remember moving the Bat-Wing plans."

"Bat-Wing?" Raining said. "Like, the superhero's plane?"

Amal laughed. "No, Raining," she said. "The Bat-Wing was a top-secret German plane that was supposed to revolutionise flight. Some people now call it the first stealth plane. But it probably wouldn't have actually been very stealthy."

"*Wouldn't* have?" Raining said.

"It was never used," Amal explained. "A few test flights crashed. That was that."

"And someone stole the plane?" Raining asked.

Dr Farah shook his head. "No, no," he said. "Someone *lost* the *plans*."

"How could Dr Heinfeld think it's your fault?" Amal said. "That's ridiculous. You never lose anything."

Amal's dad was the sort of man who liked a place for everything and everything in its place. That's why he became an archivist to begin with.

"Ridiculous or not," Dr Farah said, "I have to find those plans. If I don't I'll lose my job."

Amal took Raining by the arm and led him into the corridor. She closed her father's office door behind them. "We need to help him," she said.

Raining nodded. "But how are we going to do that?" he asked.

"With some help from our friends," Amal said. She pulled her phone from her pocket and her thumbs flew across the keys as she typed. *My dad needs our help. Come to A&S ASAP!*

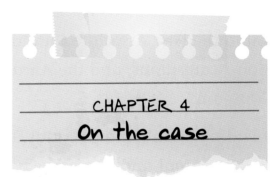

CHAPTER 4
On the case

In another part of the city, thirteen-year-old Clementine Wim rode her silly old bicycle as fast as it would go. The thing was probably older than her grandmother, but she took good care of it, and it served her well.

Today Clementine enjoyed the midday sun that hung over the tree-lined path between the Capitol City Museum of Art, where her mother was the Executive Assistant to the First Associate Curator of Collection Acquisitions, and the Air and Space Museum.

Clementine hadn't known Amal Farah for very long. Amal and her father had only moved to Capitol City a few weeks earlier. But Clementine was a very good judge of people, and she knew right away that she and Amal would become close friends. The fact that her two dearest friends, Raining and Wilson, had also taken so quickly to Amal only confirmed that belief.

And now Amal had sent an urgent-sounding message to her and Wilson. It sounded as if her father was in some kind of trouble, and she needed their help.

Clementine had immediately dropped everything – literally! She'd dropped a paintbrush she'd been using in the museum's warehouse to turn some old shipping pallets into art, and started cycling.

As she pulled into the Air and Space Museum's car park, Clementine spotted Wilson Kipper climbing out of his mother's little blue car.

"Hi, Clemmy," Wilson called. He gave her a little wave as she approached. "How's it going?"

Clementine was not a fan of nicknames, but Wilson was a good friend, so she let him get away with it. "Hi, Wilson," she said. "You must have got Amal's message too, eh?"

Wilson nodded. "Yes, I did," he said. "Sounds as if Amal's got a mystery to solve."

"Oh?" Clementine said. "Have you spoken to her?"

"No," said Wilson, "but what else could it be? That's what we do, isn't it? We solve mysteries."

* * *

A few minutes later, the four friends were gathered in the museum's canteen eating sandwiches and drinking fizzy drinks. Dr Farah was so distracted by his missing-plans problem that he didn't seem to mind buying lunch for four children instead of just two. In fact, Amal wasn't sure he'd even noticed.

After paying for their food, Dr Farah had excused himself and gone to sit at a table alone. Amal glanced over at her father. He seemed deep in thought as he stared down at his tray, mumbling to himself and going over everything he'd done that morning.

"He's desperate," Amal said.

"We'll get to the bottom of this," Wilson said. "We need to work out who'd want to take the plans."

"You think someone stole them?" Amal asked.

"Don't you?" said Clementine. "You must if you called us to come here. It's a mystery, isn't it?"

Amal shrugged. "It's a mystery how my dad could have lost anything," she said.

"He's beyond organized. I just can't believe it's true."

"Maybe someone else lost it," Raining said. "Who else would have been in the archives today?"

"Just Dr Heinfeld," Amal said.

Clementine sat up straight. "Has anyone talked to Jimmy yet?" she asked. "He's head of security. Perhaps he can check the security camera footage."

"Great idea," Amal agreed, standing up from the table. "Let's go and ask him. There's no time to waste."

* * *

"No, no, no," said Jimmy, shaking his head and crossing his arms across his chest. "I can't just pull up the tapes for everybody who asks."

"Does it happen a lot?" Wilson asked curiously.

"You're the second request I've had today," Jimmy told them.

"But it's possible that something was stolen," Amal said. "And my dad is being blamed!"

"Dr Farah?" Jimmy said, sounding concerned. "But that's crazy. Your dad would never do anything like that."

"We know," said Wilson. "So let us see the footage, and we can prove that he didn't."

"I wish I could, kids," Jimmy said. "But the truth is, I'm not allowed to show anyone the footage without an order from the police department."

"No one?" said Amal.

"Well," said Jimmy, shifting in his chair a bit, "Dr Heinfeld, of course. She's one of the bosses. And the board of directors could ask for anything, really. Those types of people."

"Bosses," Clementine said, and Jimmy nodded.

"Sorry, kids," said Jimmy. "I wish I could help."

Using his beefy arms and large belly, the security guard ushered the children towards the door of his office and out into the corridor. Then he shut the door firmly behind them.

"Maybe we should go to the police," Wilson suggested, "if that's what it takes to review the footage."

"Or we can ask the bosses, like Jimmy said," Clementine pointed out. "How about Dr Heinfeld?"

Amal and Raining exchanged a glance. "I don't know if we should bother her," said Amal. "She was in a pretty horrible mood earlier."

"Still," Clementine said, "you heard what Jimmy said. If Dr Heinfeld asked, he'd show her the footage. Don't you think she wants to know what happened as much as we do?"

Amal thought that walking up to her dad's angry boss and asking for a favour sounded like the scariest thing she could

imagine. But what choice did she have?
She had to do it for her dad.

"Okay," Amal agreed. "Let's get this
over with."

The four friends headed back to the management offices. They passed by museum exhibits almost without noticing: a shuttle, a lunar module, a rocket model, antique planes and a huge moon landscape. They passed one thing, though, that they all noticed.

"Ruthie Rothchild!" they all said together as a girl hurried past, hugging her bright red backpack.

Ruthie skidded to a stop. "Oh," she said with an irritated sigh. "It's you four. What do you want?"

They all knew Ruthie in the same way they knew each other – through the network of museums in Capitol City. Ruthie's father was the Director of Temporary Exhibitions at the Capitol City Museum of the Postal Service. None of them had ever been to that museum, but Ruthie turned up at their parents' museums all the time.

"We don't want anything," Amal said, stepping forwards. They were the same age, and Amal knew that Ruthie would probably be in some of her classes in the autumn. She wasn't looking forward to it.

"What are you doing here, anyway?" Amal continued. "You're not supposed to take your bag into the museum. You should have handed it in at the front desk when you came in."

"I'm going there *now*," Ruthie snapped. "So there." Then she hurried off, apparently toward the baggage counter.

"She's up to something," said Wilson suspiciously as they watched Ruthie hurry away from them.

"She's always up to something," Clementine agreed.

The four stood there for a moment, thinking it over, and then hurried on to Dr Heinfeld's office.

* * *

"She's not here," Amal said, peering through the narrow window of Dr Heinfeld's office. It was dark inside. "I wonder where she's gone?"

"It doesn't matter," Clementine said with a shrug. "We don't need her anymore anyway."

"We don't?" Wilson said, sounding confused. "Why not?"

Clementine shook her head. "Because," she said, "Ruthie did it. Isn't that obvious?"

Clementine might not have had a good reason to suspect Ruthie – other than their history. Of the four friends, Clementine had known Ruthie the longest.

Even though Ruthie was a couple of years younger, she and Clementine had grown up together. Ruthie had always been bigger and nastier.

When they were aged four and six, Clementine had invited Ruthie to paint with her. Ruthie thanked her by tipping a whole bottle of paint on Clementine's artwork.

When they were nine and eleven, Clementine had invited Ruthie to her birthday party. Ruthie came and knocked the cake off the table – and right onto Clementine, who just happened to be wearing her favourite dress.

"Oops!" Ruthie had said, pretending it was an accident. Their parents had believed her. Clementine had not.

And just a few weeks ago, Clementine had finished her final project for her sculpture class. She'd loved it – until Ruthie came along. The younger girl had clenched her hand into a mean little fist and punched Clementine's copy of Rodin's *Thinker* right in the face. The still-soft clay had been squished out of shape, and after that, Clementine's project didn't look much like a thinker anymore.

"Clemmy," said Wilson, "are you sure you're not just assuming the worst about Ruthie because … well …"

"Because she *is* the worst?" Amal finished for him.

"Yes, she *is* the worst," Clementine agreed. "But she also had a bag. We should search it."

"We can't just go around searching people's bags," Amal said.

"Not *people*," Clementine argued. Her voice was quiet, but still a little angry. "Just Ruthie."

Amal smiled and put an arm around her friend. "If she stole the plans," she said, "we'll find the clues to prove it. I promise."

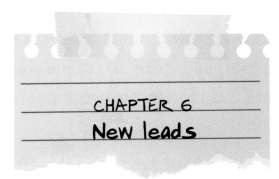

CHAPTER 6
New leads

The four friends tracked Ruthie down again in the canteen. She was sitting at a table alone, but this time, her backpack was nowhere to be seen.

"I'll handle this," Amal said. Since it was her father in danger of losing his job, she might as well be the one doing the questioning.

Amal marched straight over to the other girl, pulled out an empty chair and plopped down at the table. "So, Ruthie," she said, "care to tell me where you were this morning between nine and lunchtime?"

Ruthie glared at Amal and then moved her chair further away. "That," she said, snarling, "is absolutely none of your business."

"It sounds to me like you're trying to hide something," Amal said. "Because maybe you were snooping around in the archives!"

Ruthie sneered. "Oh, please," she said. "Why would I waste my time waiting around there? I don't even know where the stupid old archives are."

"Ha!" Amal said. "A likely excuse."

Ruthie just rolled her eyes. "Stop behaving as if you're the police or something," she said. "I can do what I want, and you can't stop me."

"Oh, yeah?" Amal said.

"Yeah," Ruthie said. "And now I want to leave." With that she pushed her chair back and stepped around Amal. She stuck her tongue out at the others and strode out of the canteen.

Wilson ran over to Amal. "I think you got her worried," he said.

Amal shook her head. "That was a waste of time. We're not going to get anything out of her," she said. "We need some new leads."

"Let's talk to Jimmy again," said Raining. "I know it sounds strange, but think about it. He had the opportunity. He's always in the museum from the moment it opens to when it closes."

"True," said Amal, "but so were you and I *and* my dad."

"But Jimmy also had the means," Raining said. "He controls the cameras, so he could have made sure they were off. Or he could have erased the video to cover his tracks."

"That is a good point," Clementine agreed.

"But why would he do it?" Wilson asked. "Ruthie might do it just because she doesn't like Amal, and she wants her dad to get the sack."

"Didn't Dr Heinfeld say the plans are really expensive?" Raining asked. "I bet Jimmy could use a little extra spending money."

"He does have new twins at home," Amal said. "It was one of the first things he told me when I met him last week. Let's go and talk to him."

Amal started walking quickly, out of the canteen, and towards Jimmy's security office, but Clementine grabbed her arm and stopped her.

"Er," Clementine said, "maybe you should let one of us handle it this time. We don't want Jimmy running off the way Ruthie did."

* * *

On the way back to Jimmy's security office, the four friends crossed through the front entrance hall. In the centre of the hall, standing near the wide, gleaming white front desk, they spotted Dr Heinfeld. She wasn't alone.

Standing beside the head archivist was a man with a long, lean face and thin, black hair, combed straight back from his forehead. He was quite a bit taller than Dr Heinfeld, but a little bit hunched over, and he wasn't dressed like the people she usually talked to. Most of them wore nice suits. This man wore jeans and a denim shirt. His hands were dirty, as if he'd just been working on a car.

"Who is that man?" Clementine asked, looking curious.

Amal shook her head. "I don't know," she replied. "I've never seen him here before. I don't think he works at the museum."

Raining took a step towards the pair, but Amal grabbed his shirt. "Where are you going?" she asked.

Raining frowned and took another step forwards. "That man looks so familiar," he said, still focused on the two adults. "I'm sure I've seen him before." Then he took another step.

"Raining," Amal snapped. "Come back here."

But her friend ignored her. Raining quickly crossed the entrance hall and walked straight up to Dr Heinfeld and the stranger. He stood right beside them, staring at the man's face. The adults didn't seem to notice him.

"Excuse me," Raining finally said. The adults immediately stopped their hushed conversation and glanced down at Raining.

"Who are you?" Dr Heinfeld asked, seeming irritated by the interruption. "Oh, you're Dr Farah's daughter's friend. What do you want?"

"I was wondering," said Raining, looking at the man, "do I know you from somewhere?"

The man shook his head. "I don't think so, kid," he said with a nervous smile.

"I'm sure I've seen your face before," Raining insisted.

"Well," the man replied, "my face does show up here and there. You might have seen it. But I don't think we've met before. Sorry, kid. "

Dr Heinfeld shot Raining another irritated look. "Why don't we go and talk somewhere a little more private?" she suggested, leading the man out of the entrance hall.

Amal, Clementine and Wilson hurried over to Raining. "Well?" said Amal. "What did they say to you?"

"Not much," said Raining. "But that man is up to no good."

"Why do you say that?" Clementine asked curiously.

"His smile," said Raining. "Something's not right about him." Raining tapped his chin with his finger. "I can't quite put my finger on it, but I know I've seen him somewhere before. I'm sure of that."

CHAPTER 7
Too close

Jimmy was sitting in his office, talking to a photo of two plump babies when Amal and her friends walked back in.

"I'll be home in a few hours, my little ginger snaps!" the security guard cooed at the picture.

"Hi, Jimmy," Amal said, snapping him out of his daydream.

"Amal!" Jimmy said, grabbing onto the armrests of his chair and sending the photo of his twins sliding to the desk. "What are you doing back here? I already told you I can't show that footage to anyone."

Amal opened her mouth to speak, but Clementine stepped in front of her. "I'll handle this," she said quietly. Then she grinned at Jimmy. He grinned back.

"Hey, Jimmy," Clementine said in her sweetest voice. "Congratulations on your new babies."

"Thank you, Clementine," he said. "That's very nice of you. I'm so proud of my baby girls."

"Maybe I can babysit for you one day," Clementine offered.

"Oh, I don't know," said Jimmy. "I'm not sure my wife will ever let those two out of her sight. She's pretty protective of our little girls."

"Of course," said Clementine. "But, Jimmy, I was just wondering. Do you stay here in your security office all day?"

"Yep," Jimmy said. "All day."

"Don't you leave to go and get some lunch?" Clementine asked, sitting on the edge of his desk. She picked up the photo of his twins and studied it.

"Well," said Jimmy, snatching the photo from her, "of course I do."

"Oh, so you *do* leave sometimes," said Clementine. "To get lunch or coffee maybe?"

"I suppose so," Jimmy said, shrugging. "If I need an afternoon snack."

"Of course," said Clementine.

"I get a little hungry around two-thirty," Jimmy admitted.

"Me too," said Clementine. "In fact, it's almost two-thirty now. Maybe I can pick up something for you in the canteen?"

"That'd be nice of you," Jimmy said. He leaned a little closer and whispered, "See if they have any chocolate-covered doughnuts."

Clementine grinned and hopped down from the desk. "Okay! Oh, one more thing, before I go," she added. "Did you leave the security office this morning at all, maybe between opening and lunchtime?"

"Hmm," said Jimmy, furrowing his brow. Then he snapped his fingers. "I did! I walked to the vending machines on the second floor."

"The ones with chocolate and peanut bars," said Clementine, nodding.

Jimmy smiled. "That's right." he said.

"And you bought a bar?" she asked.

"Two," Jimmy confessed, blushing a little bit.

Clementine looked around the room for a rubbish bin. She spotted one in the corner and shot a glance at Wilson. He nodded and hurried over to the bin. Reaching in, he pulled out two bright red-and-yellow sweet wrappers, their insides stained with chocolate, and held them up.

"Okay, Jimmy," said Clementine. "I'll drop in with a doughnut for you a little later. Bye!"

As they left Jimmy's office, Clementine shrugged. "His story adds up," she said. "He went and bought some chocolate."

"But that doesn't mean it's *all* he did," Wilson pointed out. "He had the opportunity to grab the plans, too."

"I suppose so," Clementine admitted. "But I think he's clean."

The four friends came to a stop behind the museum's front desk. The ticket collector was on the phone at the far end. Right in front of them were a dozen cubbyholes, some with bags in them.

Amal elbowed Clementine gently. "Recognise any of those?" she asked.

Clementine scanned the collection of bags. One of them, bright red with a green tag and purple drawings on it, was familiar. "Ruthie's!" she declared.

Amal nodded.

Clementine opened her eyes wide. "Should we?" she said. "It doesn't seem right."

The ticket collector wasn't paying any attention to the children standing near by.

"We have to," Amal said. "We have to solve this crime."

"We don't even know if it *is* a crime," Raining pointed out.

"It must be," Amal said. Before anyone could stop her, she darted behind the desk and grabbed Ruthie's bag. Then she slung it over her shoulder and hurried off. Her friends followed until they were safely out of sight, sitting in the shadow of the lunar module.

Amal unzipped the bag and tipped the contents onto the floor. There were books, a hand-held video game, a make-up bag, as well as brochures and leaflets from every museum in the city.

"Wow," Amal said. "Why does she need so much *stuff*?"

They spread everything out, hoping to find something that looked like Bat-Wing plans. But nothing did.

"This looks familiar," said Raining. He grabbed a glossy brochure and held it up for them to see. "You've got the same one in your pocket."

"Oh, yes!" said Amal. "Flying Funland."

Raining flipped it over. "I've got it," he said. He pointed at a little picture on the back. It was a man's face.

"Him?" Amal asked. She shrugged. "Who is he?"

"That's Francis," said Clementine, craning her neck to read the photo's caption. "As in Francis's Flying Funland."

Raining nodded. "*And* he's the man your dad's boss was talking to in the entrance hall!"

"What's he doing here?" Amal said.

Raining scanned the brochure. All the rides at the amusement park were based on spaceships and planes from over the decades. Some looked like brand-new shuttles, and some looked like antique flying machines. "He doesn't have the Bat-Wing," Raining pointed out.

"So?" said Amal.

"So maybe he'd like to," said Clementine. "And he needs the plans to make one."

Amal and Wilson nodded. The four sleuths were on to something.

"Now all we have to do is track down this Francis person and prove our theory," said Amal.

Just then, a familiar voice echoed through the room. "I'll be ready in a minute, Mum!" a girl called. "I just have to get my bag from the front desk!"

"Ruthie!" the friends exclaimed together.

As quickly as they could, the four of them crammed everything back inside Ruthie's bag. They ran over to the front desk.

Then they saw Ruthie – heading straight for the ticket collector to get her bag. She was between them and the desk. They'd have to get past her without letting her see that *they* had her bag.

Amal quickly passed the bag to Raining, who hurried to the edge of the room. Clementine called out, "Hey, Ruthie!"

The other girl spun around and sneered at Clementine. "What do *you* want?" she snapped.

"Er…" said Clementine. She tried to keep her eyes off Raining as he crept towards the front desk. "I was just wondering … if you … er … had a nice time at the museum today. Was it fun?"

Ruthie rolled her eyes. "You're being even stranger than you usually are," she said, turning her back on her.

Before Ruthie could discover Raining, Amal ran over and stood in front of her. "Hi, Ruthie," she said, blocking the other girl's path and view of the desk. She frantically waved to Clementine to hurry up and go around them.

Clementine ran past them.

"Did you see the … er … space shuttle?" Amal asked.

"Obviously," said Ruthie. She went to step past, but Amal blocked her. "Could you please move! I need to get my bag."

"How about the Martian skeleton?" Amal asked.

"The what?" said Ruthie. "There's no Martian skeleton here ... is there?"

Meanwhile, Clementine grabbed Ruthie's bag from Raining and hurried to the front desk. But the ticket collector was off the phone now, and she was watching the whole scene very closely.

"Hello," Clementine said sweetly.

"Hello," said the ticket collector, trying not to smile.

"I'd like to leave this bag, please," Clementine said.

"*Your* bag?" the ticket collector asked.

"Er..." Clementine said, "something like that."

"I see," said the ticket collector. "How about I slip it back into this cubbyhole? The same one it was in when your *friend* dropped it off a couple of hours ago?"

"Great!" said Clementine. "Sounds good to me." She looked over her shoulder. Amal had done a great job slowing her down, but now Ruthie was heading her way.

"Oh, got to go!" said Clementine as she hurried away. "Thanks!"

She joined her friends and watched as Ruthie went up to the counter. The girl glared at Amal, Clementine, Wilson and Raining, but she didn't seem to know what they'd done.

"Can I have my bag, please," said Ruthie. "It's bright red with a green label."

"Oh, I know just the one," said the ticket collector.

The four friends sighed with relief as they pushed through the museum's front door. As soon as they were outside, they burst out laughing.

"Wow," said Amal. "*That* was close."

"*Too* close," said Clementine.

"But it was worth it," said Raining, "even if she didn't take the plans."

"Right," said Amal. "Because now we know who *did*."

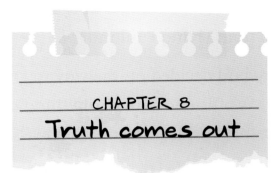

CHAPTER 8
Truth comes out

"Dr Heinfeld?" Amal said, sticking her head into the boss's office. "I'm sorry to bother you, but have you got a minute, so we can talk?"

The doctor sighed at the four children standing in her doorway. "No, not really," she said.

"It's really important," said Amal. "Do you know how we can get in touch with Francis from Flying Funland?"

They had decided on the way to Dr Heinfeld's office not to say anything about their suspicions, just in case they were wrong.

"How would I know?" Dr Heinfeld asked angrily.

"Weren't you talking to him near the entrance hall earlier?" Amal asked. "We saw you with him."

"The tall, thin man in jeans," Raining added. "He looked a bit like a car mechanic."

Dr Heinfeld stood up and paced behind her desk. "Oh, that man," she said. "I didn't know his name." She shrugged and then sat down. "He was just a museum visitor asking about an exhibition."

"Oh," said Amal. "It looked as if you knew him."

"Well, I didn't," said Dr Heinfeld. With that, she closed the door in their faces.

"Well, that was rude," Amal muttered under her breath.

"Now what do we do?" said Wilson. "Can we go to Flying Funland to find him?"

"Now," said Clementine, "it's doughnut time."

"What?" said Amal. "You're hungry?"

"No," said Clementine, "but I promised Jimmy."

* * *

"There were two chocolate-covered doughnuts left," Clementine said when they walked back into the security office. "I bought both, just in case."

"Oh, thank you," Jimmy said gratefully. He grabbed the bag and peered inside, licking his lips eagerly. "I'm so glad you turned up when you did. Normally I'd have my snack from home for the afternoon."

"Did you forget it today?" Clementine asked.

Jimmy took an enormous bite from a doughnut – so big that there was only half left. "No," he said. "I never forget a snack. But this morning Dr Heinfeld came by – I mentioned that, didn't I?"

"I don't think so," Clementine said, glancing at her friends gathered near the security office door.

Jimmy finished the first doughnut. "Not really important," he said. "She was here. She said she forgot to eat breakfast and took my extra banana muffin."

"So she just took it?" Clementine said. "How rude."

"Well, she *is* the boss," Jimmy replied with a shrug.

"True," said Clementine. "Does she drop by to steal muffins a lot?"

Jimmy shook his head. "No," he said. "But she wasn't here just for the muffin. She wanted to look at some security footage first."

"Why?" Clementine asked, sensing she was onto something. Her friends moved closer to the desk.

"Who knows?" said Jimmy, shrugging. "As I said, she's the boss."

"Well, what did she watch?" Clementine asked.

"A few minutes from the archives camera, I think," said Jimmy.

"What was on the footage?" asked Amal, leaning closer.

"I don't know," said Jimmy. He grabbed the second doughnut. "She asked me to go for a walk while she watched. That's when I got my chocolate bars."

"I see," Clementine said thoughtfully. "Enjoy your doughnuts."

"Thanks," said Jimmy, his mouth full and no sign of the doughnuts.

Clementine and her friends hurried away from the office. "That's all the evidence I need," she said.

Amal nodded. "Should I tell my dad?" she asked. "He'll be so relieved."

"We'd better prove it first," Wilson pointed out.

Raining nodded. "I think Francis will have the proof," he said.

"We still have to find him," Wilson pointed out.

"And we don't have long to do it," said Amal. "The museum will close soon, and if those plans aren't back by the end of the day, my dad will lose his job."

Wilson checked the watch he wore on his wrist – it had a picture of a pterosaur on it. Nearly everything he owned had a picture of a pterosaur on it. "My mum will be here soon to pick me up," he said.

"That's perfect," said Amal. "So you think she can give us all a lift somewhere?"

* * *

Dr Kipper was happy to drive the four of them anywhere, especially if it meant helping Dr Farah. In no time at all they arrived at Francis's Flying Funland, and the four sleuths piled out.

From the parking lot they could see huge models of the planets with an exciting roller coaster ride zooming around each one. There were spinning plane rides and bouncing lunar module rides.

"Wow!" said Amal. It was amazing.

"I'll wait right here," Dr Kipper called after them. "Don't be too long, please."

They ran to the front gate. "Excuse me," Wilson said to the ticket seller. "We need to speak to Francis right away. It's an emergency."

"Sorry," said the man in the ticket booth. "I can't let you in without a ticket."

"How much?" Clementine asked.

"For four of you?" he said. "That'll come to two hundred and forty dollars."

"We haven't got that much money!" Amal exclaimed.

"Sorry," said the ticket seller. "No money, no tickets."

Just then, a pickup truck screeched to a stop in a nearby parking space marked "Reserved." The man they'd seen at the museum earlier climbed out carrying a brown folder under his arm.

"Francis!" Raining shouted, running over to him.

"You again," said the man. "Why do you keep bothering me?"

"We don't mean to annoy you," Amal said as the other three ran up to the man as well. "But we're trying to help my dad. He's in a lot of trouble."

"I'm sorry to hear that," said Francis, "but I don't see how I can help you."

"He's in trouble," said Clementine. "And I think it's because of that file under your arm."

Looking surprised, Francis pulled out the file and opened it. "I don't understand," he said. "I bought these from a very stern woman at the Air and Space Museum."

"That's what we thought," said Amal. "But she wasn't supposed to sell them. They belong in the archives at the Air and Space Museum."

"And now she's blaming Amal's father because they are missing," said Raining.

"He's going to lose his job," Amal said.

"I see," said Francis. "We'd better get back to the museum and get this sorted out right away."

Dr Kipper stuck her head out of the driver's side window. "Kids," she called, "we should get going. The museum will close soon."

"I'll follow your car," said Francis. "Let's hurry."

CHAPTER 9
Solved

Dr Heinfeld and Dr Farah were both in the entrance hall when the children got back to the museum. Dr Farah was frowning and holding a box filled with all the personal items from his office.

With them stood a tall elderly man wearing a very nice suit. He had a bushy white moustache and crazy white hair, and he was shaking his head sadly.

"That's Mr Janovic," said Amal quietly. "He's the chairman."

"I'm afraid I see no other option, Dr Farah," said Mr Janovic. "I have no choice but to fire you."

"Sir," said Dr Farah. "If you'll just – "

"Not another word out of you," said Dr Heinfeld, cutting him short. She grabbed Dr Farah's elbow and started pulling him towards the door, but the four friends blocked her way.

"Excuse me!" the head archivist said. "Move aside."

"I don't think so," Clementine said, crossing her arms in front of her chest.

"Sir," Amal said to Mr Janovic, "you're firing the wrong person."

"Is that so?" the chairmain said. "And whom should I be firing?"

"Ask Francis," Amal said. She stepped aside, and Francis walked up to the chairman.

"Sir," Francis said, "I'm afraid I'm involved in this." He handed over the brown folder.

Mr Janovic, a bewildered look on his face, opened it up. "Oh my goodness!" he said. "The missing plans! Where did you get these?"

Dr Heinfeld ran over and grabbed the plans out of his hands. "How dare you!" she snapped at Francis. "You stole these from the museum when you were here earlier, didn't you?"

"She's lying!" Wilson exclaimed.

"She's the one who stole them," said Raining.

"And she erased the video in the security office," Clementine added, glaring in Dr Heinfeld's direction.

"And she framed my dad," said Amal, "and sold the plans to Francis for his amusement park."

Francis nodded. "I'm afraid that's right," he said regretfully. "If I'd known they were stolen, I never would have bought them."

"I see," said Mr Janovic. "Is this true, Dr Heinfeld?"

"Of course not!" she said. "It's totally ridiculous."

"I will get to the bottom of this," Mr Janovic said. "Meanwhile, Dr Farah. You're unfired."

"Thank you, sir," said Dr Farah. Leaning down, he kissed his daughter on the cheek. With a grateful smile, he hurried away to unpack.

Just then, Jimmy came out of the security office. "We're about to close, everyone," he said. "Oh, Dr Heinfeld. Did you enjoy that banana muffin?"

"What banana muffin?" Mr Janovic asked.

"The doctor had one of my muffins," Jimmy explained, "when she stopped by this morning to look at the security video footage."

"So you *did* erase the video!" said Mr Janovic. He fixed Dr Heinfeld to the spot with an even, icy stare. "*You* are fired, Dr Heinfeld."

Dr Heinfeld's mouth dropped open in shock. "You can't be serious! You're not taking the word of four children and one security guard over *mine*, are you?" she said, aghast.

"I most certainly am," Mr Janovic said. "Clean out your office right now. Our *new* head archivist, Dr Farah, will be needing it."

With that, the chairman strode away, and Amal, Clementine, Wilson and Raining cheered.

Dr Heinfeld, however, was furious. She stamped her high-heeled shoe on the ground so hard that the heel broke. When she tried to storm out of the lobby, her uneven walk, on just one heel, had everyone laughing.

"Another mystery solved," said Wilson proudly.

"And we solved it before closing time," Clementine added.

"Tomorrow you children should come down to Flying Funland," Francis said.

"We'd love to," Amal said. "But we can't afford those tickets. The museums are free for us."

"Don't worry about the price," said Francis. "You know the owner!"

About the Author

Steve B.

Steve Brezenoff is the author of more than fifty middle-school chapter books, including the Field Trip Mysteries series, the Ravens Pass series of thrillers and the Return to Titanic series. In his spare time, he enjoys video games, cycling and cooking. Steve lives in Minnesota, USA, with his wife, Beth, and their son and daughter.

About the Illustrator

Lisa W.

Lisa K. Weber is an illustrator currently living in California, USA. She graduated from Parsons School of Design in 2000 and then began freelancing. Since then, she has completed many print, animation and design projects, including graphic novelizations of classic literature, character and background designs for children's cartoons and textiles for dog clothing.

GLOSSARY

astronaut someone who travels in space

astronomy study of stars, planets and space

brochure booklet, usually with pictures, that gives information about a product or service

donor someone who gives something, usually to an organization or a charity

exhibition display or show that is usually open to the public

gracious very polite in a way that shows respect

planetarium building with equipment for reproducing the positions and movements of the Sun, Moon, planets, and stars by projecting their images onto a curved ceiling

stealthy secret and quiet

viable workable or capable of succeeding

DISCUSSION QUESTIONS

1. Do you think it was fair for Amal and her friends to immediately suspect Ruthie? Talk about why or why not.

2. Were you surprised to find out who the real culprit was? Talk about who else you might have suspected if you were on the case.

3. Would you ever want to travel into space? Why or why not? Discuss the reasons behind your decision.

WRITING PROMPTS

1. Write a chapter that continues this book. What happens after the children solve the mystery of the missing plans?

2. There are several museums in the Capitol City network. Write a paragraph about which one you think would be most interesting to visit and why.

3. Amal and her friends each have their own interests and hobbies. Write a paragraph about one of your hobbies or interests. What do you enjoy about it?

AIR AND SPACE INFORMATION

The National Space Centre opened in Leicester in 2001 and is the UK's largest visitor attraction dedicated to air and space exploration. At the space centre you can take part in a journey through history, encounter real rockets, see a dog spacesuit and take a look at genuine moon rock!

Space Exploration:

NASA is an acronym that stands for National Aeronautics and Space Administration.

NASA became operational on 1 October 1958 – one year after the Soviets launched Sputnik 1, the world's first artificial satellite.

The International Space Station is the largest artificial body in orbit and is approximately the same length and width as a football pitch. It is so large, in fact, that it can often be seen from Earth without a telescope.

Aviation Facts:

The Wright brothers, Orville and Wilbur, are credited with inventing and building the world's first successful aeroplane and making the first controlled, sustained human flight on 17 December 1903.

The **Wright 1905 Flyer**, the first practical aeroplane, flew for 33 minutes and 17 seconds, covering a distance of 20 miles, on 4 October 1905.

MUSEUM MYSTERIES

Check out the Capitol City sleuths'
next adventure and help them solve
crime in some of the city's
most important museums!

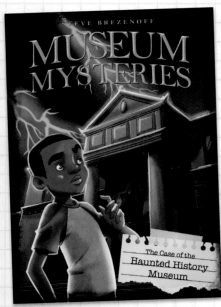

The Capitol City Natural
History Museum is
haunted — or at least that's
what someone wants people
to think. But Wilson Kipper,
son of the museum's head
paleontologist, knows better.
When the strange occurrences
turn dangerous, the museum
is forced to close its doors.
Can Wilson and his friends
get to the bottom of things,
or will the Natural History
Museum be closed for good?